Lost a

Prologue

She squeezed the handle of her saddle leather duffel bag, trying her best to look as calm as possible. After all she had done this numerous times.

She scolded herself for the attention she drew as she anxiously tapped her foot on the floor in front of her.

The Spanish speaking couple in front of her was speaking with the customs agent about their trip to Belize. They were there for a wedding and were speaking in rapid, excited Spanish.

Lena translated what they were saying in her head. She tried anything at that point would help her relax; help her remain calm as she handed her passport to the handsome agent.

"How are you doing today, Ma'am?" he asked as he glanced at her picture and smiled at her lovely face.

"I am well", she said returning his warm smile. He reviewed her paperwork and stamped her passport as he pointed her towards the security line.

She took another deep breath. This was the most important part of her trip; passing through security.

She could feel the sweat trickle down the side of her face, as she placed her bags in the small containers and walked towards the scanners.

She could hear Rafael's voice in her head, "Be calm, all will be fine if you simply remain calm". She took a deep breath, thinking about him.

Lena raised her arms towards the sky as instructed by the TSA Agent. Once the body scanner completed its cycle she finally breathed again.

"Whew" she said to herself as she gathered her items. She was homebound. Lena couldn't wait to return home to her sister and family.

She missed Rafael already, but she knew in her heart that she would see him again soon. She smiled to herself, still swooning about the previous night.

He took her on a ride of her life. She saw stars and she would never forget it. He romanced her and then took her to the beach and made love to her passionately.

Her body responded to her thoughts of Raphael. She longed to have him close to her. To smell the mint and lavender in his long locs. She was obsessed with this man. Had been from the day they met.

He was her lover after all.

She suddenly felt the strong grasp of cold hands on her body. Lena gasped as she was swiftly and forcefully turned around. "What are you doing?" she demanded as she faced the stern glare of a security agent.

"Ma'am could you please come with me?" The agent grabbed Lena and began directing her to a large steel door without waiting for her response. Lena nearly passed out as she was dragged back to the white walled room.

"What do you want?" she asked in Spanish as the Agent snatched her bags from her hand and threw them on the table. He pointed to the chair and instructed her to be seated.

"I think you know exactly what we are looking for, Ma'am!" he said as four additional agents joined him in the room.

She was caught. As they stripped her of her clothing, Lena cried out in anguish. "Stop!" she screamed as they roughly groped her body, searching for the contraband.

She collapsed on the floor in tears. The thoughts that swirled through her mind were maddening. This was her sixth time making this trip and now, the moment that she decided never to do this again, she gets caught?

Lena couldn't believe the situation she got herself into. Images of her sister and her parents flooded her mind as the tears continued to fall.

She knew that she would never see her family again and they will never know why.

"Where is it?" the police officer demanded as he tapped the stick on the table trying to get her attention.

She shook her head violently; she couldn't tell them what she was carrying. She continued to plead with them to take her to the embassy. "I'm a US citizen.

"What were you planning to do here?" the police offer asked as he walked towards her, boring holes in her forehead with his eyes.

She silently prayed that these people wouldn't kill her. Especially once they found out what she had on her. The thoughts raced through her mind, trying to tell her what to do next.

She needed some serious help at the moment. These were one of the moments when she wished that her mind was as crafty as her sister's.

"Please take me to the embassy!" she screamed in anger as the police officers continued to assault her with a barrage of kicks and slaps.

They would kill her for sure. She yelled, "NO!" as they continued to pummel her with assaults, demanding that she answer them.

Chapter 1

Eliza danced around the kitchen as Hall and Oats pumped through her Bose speaker system. The music calmed her nerves as she continued chopping the green peppers for the enchiladas.

She was preparing dinner for a special someone and it all had to be perfect. He loved the way she cooked and she wanted to surprise him with her favorite meal.

The aroma filling her small white rambler was intoxicating. She loved cooking. The colors, the smell the taste, there was nothing like it. Her dream was to become a chef. She studied at a lovely culinary school near her childhood home in South London.

It felt like a lifetime ago. Now, she was living in a small suburban Maryland town, raising her teenage son on her own. She was working as an Actuary in the federal government and as much as she hated the hustle and bustle, she was proud of her accomplishments.

Her parents wanted her to get a job that could feed her and Garcon. They urged her to stay in London with them, but she knew that in order to give her son a better life, she had to move.

A new world was calling her. As the memories flooded her brain, she questioned if she made the right decision. The ringing phone interrupted her thoughts.

She grabbed her cell phone as she absently tossed the last of her peppers in the skillet.

"Hello" she said turning the music down. "Eliza, I really need your help" she heard through the line crackling. She immediately recognized the terrorized voice on the other end.

It was her younger sister, Lena on the line.

"Lena!" she exclaimed as the line went dead. Eliza's hands began to tremble as she tried to redial the phone number but she kept receiving the same recording. "This number cannot be connected".

After her ninth futile attempt she tossed her phone on the couch and cried helplessly as she thought about her sister being in turmoil.

She sat in the fetal position with her arms wrapped around her legs, trying to console herself.

Just as she did when she was a child.

For as long as she could remember she was responsible for her younger sister.

She managed to get her sister out of their crime-ridden town to bring her to a happier life. She couldn't imagine her sister falling into any trouble

What could have happened to Eliza?

Chapter 2

Mynah sat at her desk, pounding away at the keyboard. Typing a monthly report for work on a Saturday night, it was all beginning to get old for her. She was bored and needed some excitement in her life.

As the thought crossed her mind, she noticed the commercial showing on the screen advertising cruises.

She thought about it to herself. It had been years since she let loose and allowed herself to be free.

Things had been rough for her over the past decade. After she escaped the monstrous conditions of a mental hospital, she landed in many different places.

She applied for jobs trying her best to fit into society and be like she had been before, a self-sufficient adult.

Her many attempts proved futile.

It always ended the same. She would do well on the interview, be offered the position and after the background check, the results were like déjà vu.

She would receive the same solemn call from an employee in the human resources department. "I apologize for the inconvenience of this all, but your criminal background is something of a concern for us".

It got to the point that she felt sorry for the poor person who had to call and tell her the news, sorrier than she felt for herself.

No one wanted to hire someone with a mental condition, especially someone like Mynah.

Years ago, she was a police detective on her way to the top. She was doing great things, working daily on her passion until one day it happened.

She was set up by the top brass at her job in Arizona. Before she knew it she was sent to a mental hospital, fighting for her life.

Mynah shook her head as she tried to free herself of the horrific images that flooded her mind. She was in a new place, starting a new life.

The backdrop of the tropical island showed signs of a new beautiful beginning. She smiled as the waved crashed against the harbor. She was literally in paradise. Nothing would remove her from this place, this position in her life.

But she was someone else here. In this new world of Belize she was Mynah Hill, a thirty year old retiree ex-pat from the United States.

She was someone who came to Belize to visit, fell in love with the island and decided to become a part of the island.

Mynah told everyone she met the story of Eva Hill. Her alter ego, the phoenix; Mynah would survive as she rose from the ashes of the person they once called Mynah.

She currently worked for the state department in Belize. A special services detective and liaison for the Caribbean Court of Justice. She loved her job and the sense of pride that it gave her.

As a police detective she was taken seriously, she had to fight with the top brass to get results and she was done with those days.

This was a new life. Mynah would be sure of it.

Mynah held on tight to the story, because she knew that if it weren't for her story she wouldn't be working anywhere and she wouldn't be sitting at her desk staring out the window as such an amazing sight.

The palm trees swayed gently in the wind as Mynah smiled to herself.

This was her new paradise and she would make the most of it.

Her second chance had presented itself in the form of a tropical island and a new life. She welcomed it all.

Chapter 3

Lena looked around the tiny prison cell, which had
most recently become her home. The rough concrete
walls and peeling paint surrounding her, reminded her
of the precarious situation she had gotten herself into.

She could hear the voices of the women in the room
next to her, and the muffled cries of other women in
the cells surrounding hers. She let out a sigh of relief,
thanking God that she had her own private cell.

She had only been confined to the prison for less than
two weeks, but to her it felt like a lifetime. The prison
cell was dark and lonely. She sat on the small wooden
pallet that lay in the floor praying daily.

Lena knew that she had to be strong to remain alive in
the prison.

She could immediately tell that she wasn't in the

States when they walked her back into the prison cell. The floors were hard concrete; the lights that hang overhead were covered in dust and barely worked. Many were shorting out overhead as everyone walked beneath them, unbothered.

The prison guards treated the women like animals. They poked and prodded with the women. At night Lena could hear their terrified screams as she tried to sleep. She knew what was going down. Lena was young, but far from a child.

Raphael told her that he would take care of her. She called him the minute she was captured. He sounded so terrified for her, it made her cry.

Raphael promised her that she would be taken care of even in the prison. She trusted in Raphael more than anyone. After all he was the man who put her on to her new job.

Although, it wasn't the greatest accommodations, he

came through on his word. She was the only inmate in the prison with her very own cell. The guards bothered the other women, but none of them worried with her.

She was in prison, but it wasn't the worst situation she had ever been in. As she sat on the edge of the pallet her mind drifted to her past.

The anxiety attack came on so suddenly, she could barely speak as she stood in front of her ex-husband. He was a tall, muscular, bear of a man and he had the ability to make her feel like a tiny insect.

An insect that he could easily and quite simply, crush.

She could feel his breath on her neck as she tried to free herself, only making him angrier. "Where have you been?" he demanded as he continued to pound his fist on the table in front of Lena.

Lena shut her eyes tightly as she braced herself for the slap. He hit her with such force; she fell to the floor collapsing on top the glass table with a loud crash.

The shards of glass punctured her skin in so many places she screamed in sheer pain. She had so many memories mirroring that one, she was haunted by them all.

Her ex-husband was a handsome, charming and noble man. He lead a church of over 2,000 members and worked as a Psychiatrist full time. She was drawn to him by his intoxicating charm and charisma.

Although, he was already a minister and Child Psychiatrist he had a way of owning an entire room. People were drawn to him like a moth to a flame. It was almost instinctively.

Little did they know he was a monster behind closed doors. He had a temper that was as ravenous as a lion's appetite and the power and might of an angry bear. There was something about him that made people fear yet adore him. He was literally revered.

When she decided to file for divorce against Moses she saw just how evil he could really be. She was estranged from her family church. The members treated her as if she were the devil himself.

Rumors of fornication, adultery and prostitution rang throughout the church. She cried as the members of the church each turned their backs on her.

Her husband encouraged their behavior. She found herself fleeing from their small town to safety in her sister's arms.

Her sister Eliza was always her rock. She came through for her like no other. Born eight years before her, Eliza took care of her younger sister as if she were her baby. Their parents worked constantly, leaving Eliza to care for her sister from birth.

They were only separated for a short time when Lena moved to Chicago from London. Eliza was still a young child and their strict Nigerian parents would not hear of sending their youngest daughter to another country alone.

They knew that Lena was responsible, but they still did not trust their daughter enough. Lena was supposed to be the one to keep the family grocery store business in their small South London town.

After she graduated from high school Lena tried to take her younger sister to the states with her, but their parents refused.

Chapter 4

Mynah dressed quickly for work. She would be starting in the legal department today and she absolutely loved working with the research and paperwork of it all.

Many of her coworkers complained about the shift moonlighting initiative their Captain imposed, but Mynah was so grateful to have a job that she didn't care about any of it.

She wanted to learn as much as possible and continue to climb the ladder there.

Belize was her new home and she was going to be great there. Nothing from Arizona haunted her any longer.

She thought back to her sleepless nights and pushed the dreams out of her head. She would find someone to help her with the thoughts and the nagging images of her tormentor.

Mynah still held memories of the way he would come

to her late at night, taunting her. He begged for her attention and then laughed as she screamed and cried out in fear.

Her last case involved something supernatural. Something she had never seen before. An incubus. A creature of the night, a demon. She was terrified of it, but as long as she didn't think about him, he didn't visit her.

She laughed at herself. He never agreed to those rules, but they kept her going. Mynah was proud to be moving forward with her life.

She hadn't seen the images of the Incubus in years. He played with her mind and taunted her for years but she promised to never give him that kind of satisfaction ever again.

She was in control of her own mind. It took years and years of therapy and hypnosis to get to this point, but she was glad to be here.

She smiled at the doorman and swung her purse on her shoulder as she walked towards her office suite. She finally felt proud of herself. After years of devastation she was rebuilding.

Chapter 5

Eliza sat through dinner with her son and boyfriend feeling completed displaced. Her mind was with her sister while her body sat at the table, smiling politely and laughing at the appropriate times.

She should have known that she wasn't doing a good job of hiding her feelings from her son. As soon as her boyfriend, David left the house he approached her with caution.

Eliza was seated on the couch with a lavender scented heating pad on her face as she tried to remove the tension headache naturally. Her son sat down next to her and slowly removed the pad, rubbing her temples gently.

"Mom, is something wrong?" he asked concerned.
"No, honey everything is fine" she responded quickly, a little too quickly.

"Okay, let's try a different approach. Mom would you

like to talk about what's bothering you?" he asked as he clasped his hands in front of him.

She chuckled at the sight of her son, the psychiatrist. The poor kid had been analyzing her for years, after inheriting his father's collection of Physician Desk Reference books and American Medical Association journals lined his bookshelf in the room.

Her son was destined to be a shrink. He had the ability to disarm people, make them feel at ease, while he peered through your eyes into your naked soul.

It crept Eliza out, but her son could read her better than a book. Her ex-husband would have been proud.

When her cellphone rang, she nearly knocked her son over to reach it. She grabbed the phone and flipped it open, screaming "Hello! LENA!" yelling into the phone. To her dismay she heard silence on the other end of the phone. "Lena is that you?" she asked crying. Then the line went dead.

She looked at her phone and tried to redial the number, but was met with the same message. "This number cannot be reached" she let out an exhausted groan.

Her son moved to her side and looked at her until she answered his question, "Okay, your aunt. Something is wrong with Eliza" she said crying as her son held her in his strong arms.

"I don't know where she is" she said helplessly. "I think she's in danger" she said as her son continued to talk to her in a soothing tone.

"You'll find her mom. I know you will. She will be okay" he said reassuringly. "Have you been to her apartment? Have you checked with any of her friends?" he asked as she thought about his questions.

She quickly jumped up from the floor and grabbed her keys. "Let's go to her house" she said as she and her son ran out of the door towards the car.

When they arrived at her sister's apartment, they used the spare key under the hanging flower pot and let themselves inside.

The tiny apartment was decorated in rich hues of reds and oranges. Lena was the eclectic sister. Her home was decorated in African prints and pictures of great leaders and philosophers hung on her walls.

She was a brilliant girl. Her degrees and diplomas hung on the wall, proudly boasting her academic achievements. Although, she was a bright young woman, she couldn't keep still long enough to hold down a full time job.

It really surprised Eliza when her sister told her about a job that she recently landed that would pay her enough to buy a new home and furnish it with cash.

Eliza didn't believe her sister, thinking that it was just another one of her flights of fanatical fancy. She brushed her sister aside and continued on.

As she looked around the apartment she wondered about the fantastic job her sister took. She said that it required travel, but she didn't tell her anything about going out of town in the next few days.

Eliza found her sister's date book siting on the table wide open. She stared at the dates that were circled with the words, BELIZE written across the top in big red letters.

According to the calendar her sister flew out of town heading towards Belize nearly a three weeks ago. "Where could she be?" she wondered. She rarely spent longer than a week in a particular place. Her calendar for the rest of the month looked clear aside from bill payments and doctor appointments.

She looked around the apartment for signs of her

sister and found none. Her sister hadn't returned from her trip to Belize.

She scratched her head thinking about the long distance phone call she received. It sounded like her sister was far away from her.

She gasped as her imagination took her to places that she didn't want to visit. What if something happened to my sister in Belize? The thought literally made her sick.

Chapter 6

Mynah sat at her desk going through the stack of inmates that required reviews in front of the Caribbean Court of Justice in Trinidad and Tobago.

She loved the trips to the Court of Justice. It was always such a beautiful yet scenic trip. The reason for the trip was usually not as noble.

The Caribbean Court of Justice heard all criminal cases for Barbados, Belize and Guyana. Since they were residents of Belize, their cases were heard in Trinidad and Tobago.

Although the weekly trip to the neighboring island was a pain in the behind, the court tried to ease the pain by covering the travel and accommodations of the legal team for both the plaintiff and defendant.

Compared to the United States, the Belize court system may have appeared outdated, but it certainly ran smoother than the American judicial system.

Being on both sides of the law in two different countries helped her see the contrast and similarities in the two.

She began entering each inmate in the system to forward over to the judicial intake department for further processing.

This was the most interesting part of her otherwise hum drum job. She was able to look at the crimes that others committed. In a way it made her feel normal. As if her issues weren't really as shocking as her Psychiatrist and therapists believed.

She would show them just how productive a schizophrenic with severe mood disorder could be when given the right job. Her diagnosis reminded her to pop her happy pills. She had to take her medication as scheduled to keep herself from relapsing. The last thing she needed was a panic attack or a psychotic episode at the place where she so skillfully lied about who she was.

They would send her ass home so quickly she wouldn't know what hit her; either that or commit her to the same place where she recently left.

She could have none of that. She was determined. As she sifted through the paperwork she looked in the eyes of each inmate's mug shot.

The poor women looked zoned out, many of them were high on whatever they attempted to smuggle out of the country. Their eyes stared back from their glassy glazed over expression showing Mynah that they had no hope.

She continued flipping and stopped when she saw the face of Lena Cummings. Lena was wearing a look of pure shock. Her eyes were bright and wide with fear as she stared through the picture Mynah was holding into her soul. Mynah took a deep breath and turned the picture upside down as she continued to read the information listed under Mynah's charges.

Mynah was being charged with smuggling contraband out of Belize. The police were still investigating the contraband, however.

She was being held at the local woman's prison while her contraband could be further analyzed.

Mynah felt a sudden twinge in her heart as she looked at the young woman's beautiful face. "You don't belong here" she said to the picture as she continued to type her name and contact information into the system.

She read over her information and noticed that Lena Cummings listed a sister in Maryland named Eliza Cummings.

She looked at the paper trying to decide what to do next. The short time that Mynah had been working for the company, she knew about the ramped dysfunction.

Mynah thought about her own family. She was alone

at the moment in her life and all she wanted was a family.

What if this prisoner had family?

Finally, she pushed the nagging thoughts aside and picked up the phone.

"Hi, I am calling from the US Embassy in Belize. I would like to speak with Eliza Cummings, if possible" she said as heard the surprised tone of the lady on the other end of the phone.

Chapter 7

Lena answered the ringing phone saying a silent prayer. She had been answering the phone with a prayer since her sister went missing.

She really had no idea what to do, but she knew deep inside her heart that something had to be done.

"This is Eliza" she responded to the woman as she listened to her speak in a monotone voice.

"Ma'am this is Mynah calling from the US Embassy in Belize. I am calling to inform you that your sister Lena has been arrested. She is currently being held in our prison", she said as Lena hung on to every word.

"Prison?" she gasped as the woman continued speaking. "Yes, we located your information on the emergency listing.", she responded as a long pause continued on the phone.

She assumed that Eliza was trying to gain composure. She couldn't imagine the fright that the young woman was under.

If only she knew the charges that her sister was facing, she would have been hysterical. That part wasn't Mynah's job. In fact, notifying the family wasn't her job either.

As she listened to the woman sob quietly on the phone, she wondered if she had done the right thing.

"Does she have an attorney? Is she safe? Can I speak to her or see her?", Eliza asked, without taking a breath.

"Yes, your sister is safe and I will give you the address and phone number to the prison where she is being held", she said sadly.

"We are going to do whatever we can to make sure that your sister remains safe as long as she is incarcerated here", Mynah said reassuringly.

"What? How long is she stuck there?" she demanded. "She has not received a court date as of yet. For now she is being held without bond until her court hearing.

After the hearing she will be remanded to the prison until her actual court date then she will be sentenced" the lady said quickly.

Eliza was beyond angry. "You say it as if my sister is going to be sentenced for a crime. What has she done?", Eliza demanded.

"I am not at liberty to divulge that information", Mynah replied. "Well someone has to tell me something", Eliza said angrily. "Please put me through to someone who can give me more information", she demanded.

Suddenly, she heard the loud click of the phone. The woman had hung up on her. Eliza's hand shook nervously as she quickly typed in the name of the prison in Belize where her sister was being held.

Eliza jumped with joy when she pulled up the website for the Hattieville Prison (Belize Central Prison). At least she had an idea of where her sister was being held.

She picked up the telephone and dialed the number to the prison, crossing her fingers as the phone rang.

A chipper female voice picked up the phone and asked how she could assist Eliza. "I am looking for a prisoner Eliza Cummings?" she asked as she waited for the lady to look for her sister's name.

"Yes, we have someone here by that name", she said

quickly. "Am I able to speak with her?" Eliza asked as the woman quickly responded.

"No ma'am. Visiting hours are Monday through Thursday 10 – 4", she responded as she quickly hung up the phone on Eliza.

Eliza quickly typed in the web address for Expedia and began searching for the next flight to Belize. Within fifteen minutes she booked and scheduled a flight for the following day and a hotel room.

"Well, I said I needed a vacation", she said to herself trying to make light of the situation. How was she going to tell her son that she was heading to Central America?

Most importantly what was she going to do once she arrived there? The questions seared a whole in her mind as she packed her things quickly and began searching for her Passport.

An image of her pulling Lena out of the ocean and performing CPR on her for three minutes, breathing life into her five year old sister.

She recalled the wave of relief that flushed over her entire body as her sister took a breath of air and began choking on the water.

Just like always she would be there to save her little sister. Eliza was going to save Lena by any means necessary.

Chapter 8

Eliza peered out the window as the plane made its

decent into Belize City International Airport. The swaying palm trees and cerulean blue water welcomed her as a long lost lover.

She smiled at the sight. Belize truly was a beautiful place. The moment she stepped off the plane she knew exactly why her sister chose this place for her vacation spot.

Eliza wondered about her sister. Mainly she was worried about her sister's health and treatment in the tiny Mexican city. She didn't call her parents. They had no idea what was going on and really they didn't need to know.

She wanted to keep them away from all of this until she had her sister back in the States.

Then she would let her sister have it. She chuckled to herself thinking about way she would light into her sister once she saw her.

The warm Caribbean breeze lifted her hair off her shoulders as she took in a deep breath. The cab driver offered to place her bags in the trunk once he helped her into the taxi.

She gazed out the window at the beautiful beaches and lovely scenery. Signs were everywhere directing visitors to the Mayan pyramids and temples. Eliza wished that her visit was for leisure.

After she secured an attorney for her sister and assured her release she would return to this lovely island and find her own piece of paradise here.

After working for years in the federal government she was ready for a change. Her son would be leaving the nest soon and heading off to college. She didn't want to be the clingy mother, hanging on to her son as he traveled to school, washing laundry and sending money gram support.

She wanted to have her own life. Eliza stared at the men who walked through the streets. Each had their own way of catching her attention. Some of the men were working outside, building or cleaning while others walked the busy streets in leisure wear.

Eliza felt the pang of loneliness as she watched the men and couples in the streets. Why didn't she have a man? Why couldn't she find a man?

Those were the questions that remained in her mind. She vowed to one day soon satisfy her appetite for pleasure and paradise. Just as soon as she reached the prison.

The cab drove along a bumpy dirt road as he continued to sing along to the Solca music pumping through the speakers of his old, smoking taxi cab.

She knew what the man wanted to ask her, but was grateful that he didn't say a word. She wondered why she was there, so she knew he was asking the same questions as he drove along towards the prison.

Eliza watched the farmers tending to the miles and miles of farmland. Some were reaping harvest, while others searched through the fields, pulling weeds.

She smiled at how slow everything seemed in the town. It made her loathe her busy life and job. She longed for this type of life.

As the cab drove along Burrel Boom Road, Eliza's heart began to beat rapidly. She couldn't imagine what her sister was going through.

She checked her bags to ensure that she had her documents. The prison required a passport and two additional forms of identification.

She wanted to make sure that she followed the rules. The last thing she needed was to travel to South America only to leave without getting to the bottom of this situation.

Eliza paid the cab driver and waved to him as he shook his head at her sadly. "Be careful, Ma'am" he said warning her as he handed her the duffel bag that she packed for her trip.

When she lifted the bag, she chastised herself for not going directly to the hotel and settling her things first. She was just anxious to see her little sister.

As she walked inside the administration building of the prison she took a deep breath. She recalled the words of her cab driver. "Good luck getting into Hattieville Ma'am. They are very strict", he warned her with a soft smile.

She enjoyed the company of the man and thanked him for his wisdom. She had never been to the prison, but she didn't have space in her heart for fear. It was time to save her sister and she didn't care what that took.

Eliza walked down the long black and white tiled hallway heading towards the reception area. A small cherub faced woman met her at the reception desk.

"May I help you?" she asked with a smile. "I am here to visit my sister", Eliza replied as the woman took her identification and typed information into the computer.

"Lena Cummings is not permitted to have visitors" she said quickly. "What?" Eliza replied. "I came a long way, Ma'am at least let me talk to her" she said pleading with the woman.

Finally, the woman nodded and stood from her position behind the desk. "I will let you speak with her, but she is not permitted to have visitors" she said reminding Eliza of their policy. Eliza nodded showing her agreement to the policy and walked behind the swift moving lady.

She was guided into an empty room with a television screen and a telephone. She looked around the room wondering what was going on.

"You can talk to her through the teleconference. Your entire conversation is recorded" she said handing Eliza a form to sign, waiving rights to be recorded.

Eliza watched as the television screen came on and the camera began to focus on a tiny dark cell. She noticed someone moving around inside the cell. Eliza grabbed the phone and said her sister's name, "Eliza!"

Just as she said the name, Lena turned to face the television screen. Eliza gasped at the face she saw. Her poor sister looked like she hadn't eaten in days. Her eyes were sunken in and her hair was sticking together as if she hadn't showered since she was arrested.

"Eliza is that you?" she heard as she watched her sister talking to the air like a psycho. "Yes, Lena are you okay? Are they treating you okay?" she demanded as her sister slowly nodded her head.

"I have to get out of her sis. Please help me" she said as she began to weep. Eliza longed to be there with her sister to hug her and let her know that she had it all under control.

"I got your back, sis" she said reassuringly as Lena smiled for the first time in weeks. "Have you been contacted by an attorney?" she asked as her sister shook her head indicating that she had not.

"I will get someone on your case, sis. No worries. I promise" she said as her sister cried and sat on the floor with her hands in her lap, rocking. Eliza knew the move all too well. That was how she and her sister coped. They used this method when their mother used to have male visitors at the house.

This kept them at peace while their mother did God knows who with whomever she chose. Eliza knew at a young age that their mother was a prostitute. She was responsible for their sister while both of her parents hit the streets.

Her father sold her mother and fed them with it. She couldn't complain. Her mother didn't. Lena was too young to remember.

Eliza walked in on her mother performing an act for her client in the living room while her father sat in the kitchen watching patiently. She didn't know what to think, but something inside of her told her exactly what was going on.

She was only ten at the time, but Eliza knew from that experience that her life would be forever changed.

It taught her two things, men weren't shit and pussy had power. If women realized the amount of power that they carried between their legs, they would be a force to be reckoned with.

Eliza knew her power. That same power fed her while she lived in Chicago for months searching for a job. It also helped her secure a life for her child, a great life at that.

As she watched her sister sitting in the dark prison cell, she knew that the power would help her get her sister out of prison.

She just had to use it on the right people.

Chapter 9

The sun was high in the sky and beaming directly on his balding head. Philippe Nan was a short stout man with a balding head and a tight smile.

He was focused intently on arriving at his office on time. He was a criminal attorney and had four appointments arranged to receive payment from his clients.

He only accepted his pay in US currency or Euros. Although he was a successful man, he was far from wealthy. This made him less successful with the ladies, that and the large egg shaped abyss on the top of his head.

Philippe was ashamed of his looks but took pride in his work. It wasn't what he looked like that got him the ladies, it was what he could do for their boyfriends, their husbands their family.

Philippe was used to being paid in other forms of currency as well, but he didn't let that information be known to the public.

He was upheld in the Belizean town and wanted his name to remain clean. As he opened the door to his business, he noticed a lovely woman standing outside the door, waiting on him.

He licked his chapped lips and smiled to himself. He assessed the woman from head to toe before he even knew her name.

She had a nice figure with long brown hair and a face of a doll. She was made up nicely and he could tell immediately that she was not from Belize. This woman who was standing in front of him was an American.

"Philippe Nan?" she asked as he approached the front door of the building. "Yes?" he asked as the woman took a cautious foot closer to him. "I really need your help. You're a criminal attorney right?" she asked as he nodded. "My sister has been wrongly accused and she is being held at the Hattieville Prison. Please can you help me?" she begged as he continued his assessment of her. Soft hands and soft lips, she was a pampered woman who knew how to care for herself.

He watched her move fluidly as he opened the door for her to walk inside. He offered her a seat and watched as she wiggled her tiny body into the seat.

Philippe smiled at the beautiful creature, praying that she had no money. He would love to make another arrangement with this woman.

"I have no money", she said as she began telling him her tale of woe. His member immediately grew erect as he thought of the possible ways that he could help her.

"Please continue" he said, encouraging her to tell her story about how badly she needed him.

Chapter 10

Eliza left the tiny legal offices of Philippe Nan feeling exuberant. She tried to fight the images that crowded her mind. Images of her having to do things for Mr. Nan that no woman should be forced to do.

She recalled the look of sheer pleasure on his face as she told her story, while he played with her breasts.

Eliza knew exactly what he was looking for and she came prepared. When she dressed to meet with Philippe her sole purpose was to seduce him into becoming her sister's attorney.

She wore a long black dress with a bright red bras and panties. She undressed as she talked to Philippe about her sister.

He couldn't keep his eyes off her. That served her purpose well, because she needed his undivided attention.

As he listened to her talk, she showed climbed on top of his desk and slowly danced for him as she allowed him to touch and fondle her supple body.

She didn't care. Sex was merely a transaction. A way

to get something for nothing. She saw her body as a weapon at times and a money machine at other times.

Her body saved her from starving, it kept her in a nice home and kept her son fed. Hell, she was prepared to send her son to college on the dollars she made from selling her body.

Sure, Eliza worked full time, but that wasn't enough to afford the lifestyle that she and her son deserved.

After she made him scream her name, Philippe told her that he would not only inquire about her sister's changes, he would arrange a face to face meeting for them.

She hailed a taxi cab and told the driver the address of her hotel room. She needed a shower and a drink. It had been a long stressful day and she was ready to relax.

As the cab pulled into the parking area of the hotel, she let out a sigh of relief. She had done a great deal of work for her sister in one day. The next task was to talk to the prosecution.

Once she found out about her sister's charges she would do whatever it took to have her sister released from prison.

She climbed into the elevator and pressed the button for the 4th floor. Just as the doors were closing she saw an arm suddenly appear through the elevator doors.

The doors opened and she stood in front of a tall, handsome man dressed in an expensive suit. She smiled a greeting to the man as he said, "Hi" to her.

After he pressed the 5th floor button on the elevator, he turned to face Eliza. "I apologize, Madame I forgot something in my room and I had to make a mad dash back into the elevator. Sorry if I frightened you", he said in a seductive French accent.

She smiled at the sensual man, allowing the smell of his cologne to permeate through her nose. She was literally intoxicated by this man.

"Richard Crabtree" he said offering his hand. "Eliza Cummings", she said as he gently shook her hand. "You in town on business?" he asked as he considered her from head to toe.

"No, I wish. I am here to help my sister", she said with a sad sigh. He turned to face her. "I am sorry to hear that. I pray that you will be successful", he said as he quickly glanced at his watch.

"Are you here on business?" she asked the nicely dressed man. "But of course. Why else would I be in Belize?" he said as they both laughed.

Suddenly, the door to the elevator opened and she stepped off. "Well it was nice meeting you, Eliza. I hope to see you again soon" he said with a large grin.

"It was nice meeting you as well. I plan to be here for a week or so. Maybe we will bump into each other again", she said as she waved to the handsome man and walked towards her hotel door.

Chapter 11

Mynah sifted through the paperwork as she continued working. Her boss was heading to Trinidad and Tobago within the next few days and she wanted to ensure that his cases were complete.

She entered the last inmate in the database, a young female accused of being a mule. Mynah stared at the sad look in her eyes, begging someone for help.

Mynah already knew what the young girls fate would be. She would be remanded to the prison for life. Although, Belize was in South America and close to Guatemala, their drug laws were quite strict.

She felt terrible about the situation, because she knew that all too often, these women are lured into their life of crime. The woman was American and was born September 22, 1990. Her story read like so many other young American women.

They come to the resort town in search of fun in the sun and find themselves lured in by the seedy underground life. It can be quite tantalizing.

The handsome men, whispering everything you want to hear in your ear. By the time they finished talking you don't want to say no to them. You are willing to go to the end of the world with them.

Then just as sudden as they meet you, they disappear; leaving you to clean up the mess. Out of the fifteen inmates that she entered in the system, six were women.

In the five months that she had been working in the division, she had witnessed a growing trend. More and more women were falling under the charm of a man and ending up in prison for life.

Mynah wanted to warn them. She wanted to launch a campaign. In fact, she suggested it to her superiors, but none of them would hear of it.

Why would they? Her boss all but pushed her out of his office when she suggested placing informational posters at the airport. All they had to do was warn the travelers that Belize was a drug free town.

Her boss scoffed at the idea, telling her that they would lose more money than he could stand. After all, he had to get his end of the year bonus. What would his wife do without another diamond?

She recalled having to go outside for fresh air after the conversation with her boss. Mynah was still struggling with her mental sanity and was susceptible to breakdowns. The last thing she wanted was to snap and end up back in the hospital.

She knew that she had to play it safe. If she could just help one woman she would be satisfied. As she stared at the lonely eyes of Lena Cummings she made an affirmation.

Lena would be the first woman that she helped. She would see to it that Lena didn't end up in the Belizean prison for the rest of her life.

She smiled at her reflection in the mirror across from her desk.

The thought of helping Lena made her enthusiastic again. She took a deep breath and let out a loud sigh. How would she begin?

Ah, she knew exactly where to start. She picked up the phone and dialed the number to her friend, Michel. He was a private investigator and would be a perfect resource for her.

Chapter 12

Eliza picked up her ringing phone as she glanced at the clock on the nightstand. It was 9:00 am on the dot. She answered the phone, wiping sleep from her eyes.

"Eliza, I have information about your sister. The Magistrate has referred her case to the Supreme Court. For some reason they are moving swiftly on your sister's case. She has a hearing tomorrow morning. We will meet at the Caribbean Court of Justice in Trinidad and Tobago.", he said swiftly.

"What happened? Why are we meeting in Trinidad?", she pondered aloud. "Your sister was appointed an attorney who has taken the case as far as it can go. Are you available to meet with me this morning? There are some things I need to show you?", he asked anxiously.

Eliza tried her best to stifle a groan. She knew what he wanted, more payment. The last thing she felt like doing with him was being in an intimate situation, but she thought about her sister and climbed out of the bed.

"Sure, I will be in your office in an hour", she said as he cut her off. "No worries, I'm in front of your hotel. I will wait for you", he said quickly.

Eliza jumped out of bed and peered out the window as she heard Philippe chuckle in the background. "Do you see me?", he asked as she quickly got dressed and washed her face to meet with him.

By the time Philippe knocked on the door, she had already brushed her teeth and threw her long locs into a high standing ponytail.

Chapter 13

As Mynah continued searching for information on Lena she grew more and more concerned. She didn't know why, but the hair on the back of her neck began to stand at attention when she reviewed her case files.

Lena had been picked up at the airport and charged with several different charges all amassing at least thirty years in prison. She gasped as she continued to read about how Lena was stopped at the airport before boarding the plane.

She searched for a source, maybe a tipster who would've let the authorities know that she was carrying contraband, but didn't see anything.

Mynah typed Lena's Passport number in the system and was able to locate additional information on the case.

An hour later, Mynah sat at her desk with her head in her hands. Something about the entire situation seemed desperately fishy to Mynah.

Lena wasn't caught by a TSA employee, none of the body scans revealed that she was carrying anything and she hadn't been x-rayed.

"How did they find the contraband?", she wondered aloud as she continued sifting through the files. Something was amiss.

The other inmates had complete files, documentation on their crimes as well as the methods for determining their guilt. In every situation, there was clear probable cause; all except one, Lena's.

Mynah was faced with a troubling decision. If she questioned the relevancy in Lena's charges, she could face opposition. Mynah couldn't allow herself to be placed in the same situation that she just got herself out of.

She knew how the government worked, when they wanted to silence someone. The things they wanted to leak were leaked, but the things they wanted to keep silent; they made sure of it.

Chapter 14

The smell of the peas and rice made her stomach growl loudly as they were ushered into the crowded room. The food sat on the long table in the back of the small cafeteria, uncovered.

As the women shuffled through the cafeteria line, they each selected a small plastic plate with their choice of food on it. No one seemed to care about the flies that carelessly congregated on top of the plantains and rice dishes.

They all shoved the food into their mouths with such passion you would have thought they'd never eaten it before. Peas and rice were on the menu every single day in that place, but who was she to complain? They were eating on a regular basis.

Judging by the thin frames of the males and females in the prison, she could tell that they had all experienced their share of rough times. She felt a soft nudge from behind as the guards urged her to continue walking.

The Hattieville prison was coed, comprising of both male and female inmates. The prison was heavily guarded and the inmates were generally kept separate aside from dining times.

Eliza felt two hands cup her ass as she reached to grab her food. She quickly turned to face the offender only to find a smiling guard winking at her. "Move it along", he said in broken English as she continued shuffling down the line.

The guards annoyed her more than the inmates. She couldn't wait until her visit with Rafael. Her man had serious pull and she knew that he would have her out of this mess soon.

She was grateful for her photographic memory, as she took a mental image of the guard. "You will be the first to die when I get out", she whispered under her breath as she continued walking toward her seat.

Lena didn't want anyone to know that she was shaking with fear inside. She hid it quite well under her deep scowl and quiet nature. The prisoners kept their distance from her and rarely tried her.

It didn't hurt that she was only one of a few Americans in the prison. Many of the others had little trust for Gringos so they steered clear of Lena.

When she initially arrived she had trouble with one inmate who currently bore a scar on her right cheek. The scar was a reminder from Lena. It also served as a warning to the others that Lena would fight back and defend herself.

Once the others saw that, they scurried off into the shadows. It also didn't hurt that her man was the man around town. Rafael was a known man in the underworld. Many feared him and she heard plenty of tales about the murders he committed; some were completely senseless.

Rafael ran a criminal organization called the Los Hermanos Guardians, roughly translated into Brother's Keeper. They ran cocaine and hashish throughout the coast of Guatemala and Belize.

The inmates whispered about her. They wondered about Rafael and the Guardians, but no one dared ask. She didn't know anyone in the place, but she knew that they already knew who she was.

Everyone feared the wrath of Los Hermanos Guardians. They were responsible for wiping out half the police force in the early 2000s, simply for a misunderstanding with the Magistrate. Nothing happened in the Caribbean underworld without their knowledge.

In fact, the Guardians were the primary reason why the Caribbean Court of Justice Drug Enforcement Unit was formed. They masterminded a multi-billion dollar criminal organization which shipped drugs in and out of the Caribbean as well as both North and South

America.

Lena loved Rafael's business sense and wealth, but it was his power that drew her in. She met him in 2010, when she first visited the Caribbean vacation spot.

She was there with a girlfriend from New York. At the time Lena was a straight laced student completing her last year in undergrad.

The only thing that mattered to Lena was pleasing her sister. She was encouraged by her sister's dedication to her.

She was interested in only her education. Her friend forced her on the trip as a way of saying thank you for the many times Lena tutored her.

It was almost as if Raphael smelled her from across the room. She and her friend Meri were enjoying themselves on the dance floor when suddenly she felt a hand on her shoulder.

Lena nearly jumped out of her skin before she looked up and stared into the sparkling eyes of Raphael Von Weiss. "Sorry to disrupt you" he said in a deep seductive tone as Lena swooned in his arms.

"I saw you from across the room and I was drawn to you", he said as she stood there with her mouth hanging open.

It was something about the way he looked at her, his accent and the smell of his cologne made her want to wrap her arms around him.

Before she knew it she was in his beach house screaming his name. By the fourth night she was hopelessly in love and willing to give him anything he asked for.

The only thing was, he never asked her for anything. He spoiled her; gave her anything she asked for and never asked for anything in return.

If only she knew then that there was a cost associated with free.

Chapter 15

Eliza loosened her grip on the coffee mug when she realized the trickle of blood running down the side of her wrist. She gasped and sat the mug on the table to examine her hand.

She was so nervous that she stuck her fingernail deep into her hand without knowing it. Philippe watched as she sucked on the wound.

"I apologize for having to trouble you, but if you want your sister to be free you are in for a long fight", he said concluding his sentence.

He had been talking to Eliza for nearly two hours, explaining the compromising situation that Lena had gotten herself into. Her head was spinning with the details. She desperately wanted to get her sister out of the prison, but it would be an uphill battle.

Her sister had numerous charges stacked against her, including drug smuggling. Each charge carried at least ten years. Her sister would remain in prison for a lifetime if Eliza didn't help her.

She couldn't imagine the horrors that her sister was suffering. Philippe told her what her sister needed to do to be free, but she knew Lena. Lena would never turn on a friend and especially not on a lover.

The man she swooned over for years, Rafael owned all of her. Rafael had control of Lena's heart, mind and now her freedom. It bothered Eliza. It made her want to turn around and climb back on the plane to the states, but what would she tell her parents?

She was responsible for her sister and she would be have her sister's back no matter what. She agreed to meet Philippe in Trinidad and Tobago the following day for Lena's trial.

Eliza had to find a way to get her sister to change her mind about testifying against Rafael. According to Philippe Rafael had women lined up around the continent.

He had several hideaways in the Caribbean that he snuck off to without a notice. Eliza questioned her sister's mental state. Why would someone give their life for a man who wouldn't even commit to them?

Eliza knew what she had to do. "Do you know a private investigator?" she asked as Philippe rubbed the stubble on her chin, trying to think of a way to lure Eliza back in the bedroom. He completely missed her question.

"What?" he asked as she stood in front of him and began undressing. "I need you to find me something on Raphael", she said as she kissed on his veiny neck and tried to ignore the smell of musk.

"Of course, my darling", he murmured as she

continued talking. "ll need you to find something to make my sister change her mind about testifying against him", she said as he continued to moan.

"Do you think you can do that for me?", Eliza asked as she took him into her mouth. She didn't need him to respond, the fact that his tiny toes had curled and his green eyes rolled in the back of his head to her all she needed to know.

He would be willing to do anything for her and that's just what she needed; a man willing to give his all to help save her sister's life.

Chapter 16

Lena's thoughts were in another place and time. She was in the arms of her lover as they talked about their future. Raphael was her best friend. He listened to her and was there when she needed him.

She recalled the first time she had to call on him. She was being hounded by the bill collectors and could barely make her rent. She stared at his phone number on her cell phone for hours deciding whether to call him or not.

The moment she heard his voice her body immediately relaxed. Within a day she was on a plane heading to Belize City to meet her lover. All she had to do for him was travel to Guatemala and pick up a package.

When she successfully delivered the first package, Raphael was happy and so was she. Lena was making nearly $30,000 per package drop and she was finally able to keep her head above water.

It drover her crazy having to depend on her older sister. She worried so much about disappointing her sister that she gave herself ulcers. She maintained an A average from elementary school throughout her senior year in college.

Lena was selected by Princeton University as a High Aptitude Scholar, earning her a free ride through college. Lena was building a stable life for herself, until it all came crashing down.

Eliza was her protector and provider for her entire childhood. She owed it to her to be a success. What would her sister say if she knew the truth about Lena?

The possibility of Lena being disappointed in her drove her to work two jobs to afford her high rise apartment in the city. She lied to her sister about having a successful career as an architect. Lena had been lying to her sister for years.

Eliza believed that Lena was a college graduate with a rising professional life. She told her sister that she traveled as perks for the job. Eliza was beyond proud of her little sister.

She wiped a tear as she recalled the look of sheer pride on her sister's face as she took in the scene from her new home in Manhattan.

Lena didn't have the heart to tell her sister the truth; that she was working as a call girl and a waitress in order to make ends meet.

Raphael helped her keep the illusion going for years. Lena had become comfortable with the process and was a pro at smuggling drugs and guns. As her man climbed through the ranks of the drug organization she was right along with him.

It disgusted Lena that she was tuck in the tiny 12 by 12 prison cell. She missed her man, he said that he would visit, but she understand why he couldn't.

He was a man on a mission and being seen within this prison wouldn't look good for his image.

She understood the world that she had grown accustomed to living in. At least she thought she understood it.

Her thoughts were interrupted by the sound of the guards approaching her cell.

Chapter 17

Eliza read the papers as large splotches of tears blurred her vision, splashing on the pages. How was she going to tell her sister this news?

She couldn't digest it all in her mind.

Lena would be heartbroken once she talked to her. She tried not to imagine the expression on her sister's face once she shared with her the information she found from the private investigator.

Lena met with him earlier during the day at a small bistro near the Hilton hotel. Ricardo Stith was a portly, unattractive man with thick black framed glasses and a limp.

He sat down next to Lena with a frown on his face as he whispered something in her ear and slid her a stack of papers. "All that you are looking for is inside of that folder", he said as he quickly stood and walked away from the table leaving Eliza seated at the table looking crazy.

After he disappeared down the street Eliza peaked inside the folder and her heart skipped a beat. There were five sheets of paper inside the folder and a cd. She shoved the contents inside her purse and got up from the table.

Eliza hailed a cab and hopped inside as she tried to envision whether the hotel had a cd player. As soon as she walked inside the hotel room she began her frantic search for a stereo. The room was in complete disarray as she continued her search.

Eliza realized that she was becoming neurotic and sat down for a moment to collect her thoughts. The paperwork and the cd awoke something inside of her that sent her composure into a tailspin.

Once she located the cd player in the bathroom of the

suite she popped the cd inside and turned the volume up high.

She listened as a conversation ensued over the telephone. "Hello, I'd like to report a hotline tip", the caller said as Eliza continued to listen to the caller describe her sister to a tee. She wondered the identity of the caller.

Whoever it was, they knew her sister well. They knew the flight number, the date and time of the flight and her complete description. Eliza sorted through the paperwork in complete shock as she read the details provided by the private investigator.

Once she put it all together she ran out of the hotel in search of a cab. The first taxi she found she told them where she wanted to go and he stalled for a moment, staring at her.

Eliza was dressed in a black silk dress and high heels. She didn't look like anyone planning to visit a notorious place such as Hattieville prison.

"Now!" she yelled as the driver stepped on the gas and drove towards the prison complex. Eliza watched as the familiar scene unfolded in front of her. In two hours the facility would be closed to visitors, she hoped that she had enough time.

Chapter 18

Lena moved quietly as she was escorted into the visiting room. She had never seen this place before. She took in the small elementary school sized desks that lined the tables and the overhead surveillance cameras.

Then she saw her, sitting at the table looking as elegant as the Queen herself. Eliza was always so regal looking. She wanted to run to her sister and melt in her arms, reliving her past disappointments and fears so that her sister could rub her back and tell her that all would be well.

Instead she allowed the guards to drag her to the corner seat and lock her handcuffs into the middle of the table. Her sister began to speak rapidly. She spoke so fast Lena had to take a deep breath and tell her to start over.

"I said, Raphael set you up Lena!" she exclaimed. Lena stared at her sister in disbelief. "What do you mean he set me up?" she demanded.

Her sister held up the papers as she spoke. "Lena who paid for your roundtrip tickets to Belize?" she asked as Lena cleared her throat trying her best to contain her composure.

"I bought it", she finally responded to her sister. Eliza looked at her shaking her head. "Oh really?" she asked sarcastically. "So you purchased the tickets for you and four friends? You balling like that Lena?", she inquired.

"What are you talking about?" Lena asked, trying her best not to jump across the table and wipe the smirk from her smug sister's face.

"Well, I hired a private investigator Lena. I'm trying to get you out of here. I found out that whoever purchased your tickets bought four additional tickets for other women on the same flight you were on", she said sadly.

"Raphael used you, Lena! You have to stand up for yourself now. Please think about Lena. Testify against him so you can have some semblance of a life", she said sadly as Lena began to wipe away hot tears from her red cheeks.

She was embarrassed by her sister's accusations. The last thing she wanted was for her big sister to have to swoop in and save the day. She wanted to do this on her own, but instead it all back fired. Her sister found out that she was a nobody, less than a nobody she was a criminal.

A criminal too stupid to realize when they are being used by someone. She allowed Raphael's smooth words and handsome face talk her into a life of crime and now she couldn't get herself out of it.

She couldn't testify against Raphael. He would have her killed before she sat in front of the Supreme Court. Things in Belize seemed well on the surface, but they were far from that where Lena stood.

Drug criminals were treated differently. They weren't given the same liberties and treatments that other offenders received.

Belize was trying to shed their image of being South America's hub of the drug underworld. They wanted to be better than that. They would make an example out of her.

What would she do?

"He had four other mules on the same flight that you were scheduled to be on!" she finally said as she wiped away angry tears.

"I don't believe you", Lena replied as she signaled the guard to remove her from the visitor's booth.

An hour after her sister's visit, Lena was on the phone arguing with Raphael. She finally decided to call him and question him about what Eliza revealed.

He denied everything her sister told her. Raphael seemed truly hurt by Lena's accusations. By the end of the phone conversation Lena found herself apologizing for her behavior and begging Raphael for his forgiveness.

Raphael said that he understood, but it was something in his tone that told Lena otherwise. Her sister's voice replayed in her head as she tried to make sense of it all.

She tossed and turned in the bed, unable to rest. When the guard walked by her cell to conduct their late night room checks she was wide awake. She sat up immediately when she heard the key inserted in the lock to open her cell.

"What's going on?" she demanded as the guards dragged her out of the cell. Lena protested, screaming and crying as four guards carried her to a small prison cell at the end of the hall.

Lena stopped screaming when she felt her tiny body being tossed on a pallet in the corner of the cell. "What are you doing? You can't leave me here!", she cried as the guards slammed the door behind her. She looked around and noticed three sets of eyes in the room.

"Well, well, well, look who's out of the palace and in the trenches with the other peasants", she heard a voice taunting her as she turned to face a woman two times her size staring her down.

"It looks like someone fell from their ivory tower", she heard as she felt her body being pummeled with punches and body blows.

Chapter 19

Eliza walked inside the hotel room and began to strip

out of her clothes. She was so angry her tears were no longer flowing, they were now burning her eyes. She wanted to fight someone. In fact, she knew exactly who she wanted to fight, her little sister.

After she gave up everything, her money and her body, that ungrateful brat didn't care enough to believe her when the truth stared her in the face.

Eliza couldn't believe her sister's selfishness. She didn't raise her to behave in the manner that she was behaving. She didn't want to hear anything bad about Raphael.

Eliza wondered how someone who worked so hard at proving how intelligent she was could be so fucking stupid.

She started talking to herself as she packed her bags. "Serves her right to be there. Maybe a few years in a foreign prison will teach her something. If she doesn't want to believe me let her see on her own", Eliza continued complaining as she threw the remaining clothes from her closet into her overnight bag.

She checked for outgoing flights to the United States through blinding tears. Her job was done. She flew over to Belize without a moment's notice to help her sister. She gave her body, money and mind to save her sister.

Sadly, she couldn't save her sister. Lena would have to save herself now. She clicked the "booked" icon on the Expedia page and typed her credit card information into the computer and clicked the confirmation button.

"Chao, Lena", she said as she confirmed her flight and checked in on the outgoing 10:0 pm flight for the evening. The red-eye flight was so expensive it cost a month worth of her salary, but it was so worth it. After years of being the responsible one, she was finally rid of it all.

Her heart hurt with guilt. She knew that her sister

needed her but there wasn't much that she could do until Lena recognized how much she needed Lena's help.

Lena paid the hotel bill and walked out the door to the awaiting car. She tried to hide the tears and swollen eyes under her shades, but it was futile. The puffy, red face gave her away.

"Is everything alright, Miss?", the driver asked as soon as she sat down in the car. "Yes", she quickly replied as she instructed the driver to head towards the airport.

She said a silent prayer, hoping that her sister would be alright.

Chapter 20

Mynah wiped the sweat from her brow as she continued reviewing the case files in front of her. She hadn't been working in Belize for long, but she knew that Lena Cummings case was completely mishandled from the start.

Lena was arrested without probable cause and held for nearly two weeks without seeing an attorney.

The records on Lena Cummings case showed that her case was immediately forwarded to the Supreme Court by the local Magistrate, but she was never removed from the local prison and transported to the CCJ in Trinidad and Tobago.

Based on a treaty established in the early eighties, detainees had to be brought before a judge within 72 hours of arrest. Mynah sifted through the paperwork, searching for documentation revealing her appointment with the judge.

Something about the case seemed so fishy to Mynah, but she continued researching and documenting. Somehow she would get the information surrounding Lena Cummings capture to her sister. She wanted to see to it that Lena walked out of the prison.

"Good morning, Eva", her boss said as he walked through the door smiling at Mynah. "Good morning sir", she replied. She still had to get used to being called Eva.

"Sir, I'm reviewing documents concerning the most recent arrests to forward to the CCJ and I found something interesting", she said holding up Lean Cummings' papers.

"Somehow Lena Cummings' case was mishandled. I am not sure that she's seen a judge yet. Her case files don't make sense", she said as her boss squinted at the paperwork and shrugged his shoulders.

"Contact Lindsey at Treasury Lane and find out what's

going on", he said over his shoulder as he walked into his office and quickly shut the door.

Her boss worked directly with the Chief Justice of Belize as a liaison. She suspected that it wouldn't take much for her to find out what she needed to know about Lena's case.

She dialed Lindsey's number and waited for the court clerk to answer. When she got Lindsey's voice mail she hung up the phone and took a deep breath.

There had to be a better way of helping Lena without being exposed. As she tapped her pencil on the desk, humming to herself the idea hit her. She could help Lena and remain anonymous.

She searched through the computer files concerning Lena Cummings and located her sisters' contact information. She found her phone number and address and let out a loud sigh.

She printed the papers out and slid them into the mailing envelope while saying a silent prayer that Eliza would find the information in time to save her sister's life.

Chapter 21

The sirens startled her waking Lena from her slumber.
She tried to move, but every turn she made she was
met with excruciating pain. Lena looked around at the
empty prison cell. What happened to the thugs who
beat her the previous night?

The prison cell door was wide open. Lena felt as if she
were in a dream. If only she could get up, she would
make a mad dash out of the cell and head to freedom.

The room was completely empty. Lena placed her
hands at her side and tried to push herself up.
"Please, don't get up on my account", she heard as
she tried to see where the voice was originating.

The guard walked inside the room and faced Lena as
she pleaded with him for help. He shook his head in
pity. "I am sorry miss. I don't know how you pissed
Raphael off, but you did", he said as his thin fingers

reached for the knife, exposing the sharp blade.

"Please don't hurt me", she said crying as the guard smirked at her. "It's not up to me", he said as he sliced at Lena's breast.

"You should've kept your mouth closed", he said shaking his head as he skillfully worked on her implants to remove the diamonds. He worked with the prevision of a surgeon.

She gasped for air as she stared at the man in sheer horror. Lena knew what he was after and seeing the knife scared the hell out of her.

"Get off of me!", she demanded trying to push him away. "HELP", she screamed trying to bring attention to her prison cell.

She wondered where the guards went. Security in the prison was always tight. The prison was usually packed with security guards and police officers.

Her mind began to race as she thought about what the guard was doing. "Oh my God!", she exclaimed as it all began to register in her mind. Raphael sold her out.

Epilogue

Philippe yawned and stretched as he opened his door to retrieve the morning paper. He returned to his seat in front of the sunroom window as he sipped on his coffee.

He had an appointment scheduled for 9:30 am with a pretty new client. She was the wife of a criminal who needed his assistance. He loved helping out those in need, especially women.

Philippe nearly choked on his coffee as he read the headline of the newspaper, "American Woman Found Dead In Cell After Prison Riot", he sadly shook his head as he read the details of the story.

Lena Cummings was found in her bloody prison cell by security guards after a prison riot erupted in her prison block. She tried to fight off her attackers, but was found with her breasts sliced open.

Philippe closed the paper and shook his head sadly as he opened the package wrapped inside the newspaper.

The smile grew on his face as he read the note and opened the bag filled with small diamonds. He rubbed the smooth rocks between his fingers as his mind drifted to the beautiful creature, Eliza. He wanted to help her save her sister, but he knew from the beginning that he couldn't.

His greed wouldn't allow it. The bounty in that tiny woman's breast implants were worth more than her life, itself. He couldn't let her survive. His children's college education depended upon it.

He accepted her sister's plea for help out of the kindness of his heart and the throbbing in his loins. Philippe knew that he couldn't tell Eliza all that he knew, it would jeopardize too much.

He recalled the desperate pleas from Eliza Cummings. She wanted to save her sister, but she had no idea how deep Lena really was in the organization.

Lena had been involved with the Lena knew too much and she was worth more dead. He couldn't tell Eliza that, though.

Instead, he gave Eliza just enough information and help with her sister to make her feel like she was accomplishing something.

As an attorney for Los Hermanos Guardians he was dedicated to his job and his family. He smiled at the picture of his wife and three children hanging above the sunroom window as he folded the paper in half and continued eating his bagel.

Made in the USA
Columbia, SC
23 September 2021